Hermit

Beverley Randell
Illustrated by Julian Bruère

Hermit Crab is at home.

She is inside a shell.

She is too big

for this little shell.

Here comes Hermit Crab.

She is looking for a **big** shell.

This shell is big.

Hermit Crab will look inside.

Oh, no!

A big hermit crab is inside.

Here comes a fish,

a big hungry fish.

He likes to **eat** hermit crabs!

Oh, help! Oh, help!

Where is a home

for Hermit Crab?

This is a big shell.

This is a good home for Hermit Crab.

She is going inside.

Go away, big hungry fish.

Go away, oh go away!

Hermit Crab is not for you.

She is not for you today.

Hermit Crab is **safe**.